The Peculiar Pig

Joy Steuerwald

Nancy Paulsen Books

Nancy Paulsen Books
an imprint of Penguin Random House LLC, New York

Library of Congress Cataloging-in-Publication Data
Names: Steuerwald, Joy, author, illustrator. Title: The peculiar pig / Joy Steuerwald.
Description: New York, NY: Nancy Paulsen Books, an imprint of Penguin Random House LLC, [2019]
Summary: Penny the puppy, puzzled by why she is different from the piglets she is raised with, uses her ear-splitting growls to chase away a snake that threatens her family.
Identifiers: LCCN 2018022831 | ISBN 9780399548871 (hardcover: alk. paper) | ISBN 9780399548895 (ebook) | ISBN 9780399548888 (ebook) | ISBN 9780399548901 (ebook)
Subjects: | CYAC: Individuality—Fiction. | Pigs—Fiction. | Dogs—Fiction. | Animals—Infancy—Fiction. Classification: LCC PZ7.1.S74435 Pec 2019 | DDC [E]—dc23
LC record available at https://lccn.loc.gov/2018022831

Manufactured in China by RR Donnelley Asia Printing Solutions Ltd.
ISBN 9780399548871
10 9 8 7 6 5 4 3 2 1

Design by Marikka Tamura. Text set in OPTI Worcester.
The illustrations in this book were hand drawn with pencil, then scanned into Photoshop and painted digitally.

In memory of my mom
and with love and gratitude to my family, friends,
and wonderful agent, Teresa

There was a different sort of piglet
in the pigpen one spring morning.

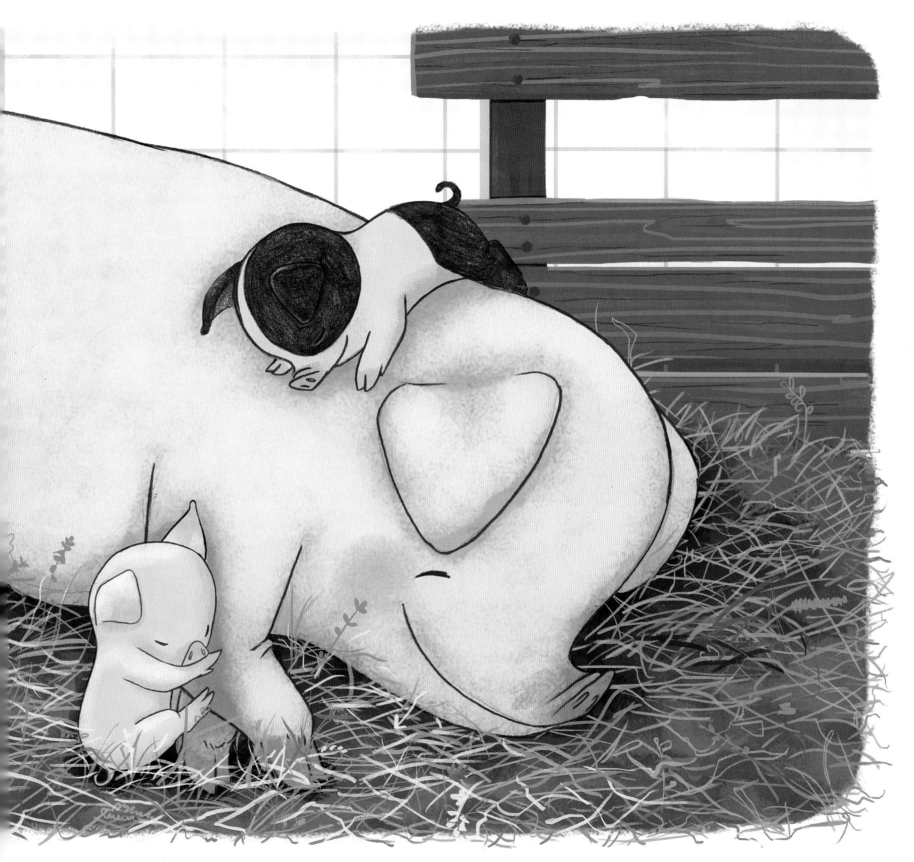

But Mama Pig didn't care.
She loved her piglets all the same.

To her, each one was special.

The other piglets were bigger and stronger and often pushed this little piglet aside,

but she was always willing
to wait her turn.

The day came when Mama Pig gave each piglet their name.

She named them . . .

Freckles

Pinky

Prudence

Patch

Scrappy

Roly

"And my shining little one."

Penny

The piglets grew bigger every day.

And Penny grew . . .

longer.

"She sure is peculiar looking!"
Scrappy told Freckles.

Penny didn't know why she was different.

But Mama Pig told her, "It doesn't matter, Penny.
I love all my little piglets the same."

As she grew, Penny started to sound different, too.

"Penny, you have a funny oink!" Freckles said.

"And it's so loud," complained Patch.

But Penny liked all the sounds she could make. She practiced her oinks, growls, and barks with Mama Pig while her sisters and brothers played in the mud.

All the piglets became good diggers.

Prudence watched Penny and told her,
"Proper pigs use their snouts to dig."

"But my paws just work better,"
said Penny.

Scrappy said, "How peculiar!"

One day, the piglets were having fun racing around the farm.

"Wow! Penny sure is quick!" said Roly.

"Even with those short little legs."
Pinky giggled.

Then something stopped them in their tracks.
It was a scary hissing creature!

All of a sudden, a fearsome sound came from deep inside Penny.

Grrrrr Ruff Ruff Ruff!!

Her sharp growls sent the creature slithering away!

"Wow!" said the piglets. "Thank you, Penny!"
Then they tried to bark just like Penny.

Penny laughed and said, "Now, those
are some peculiar growls!"

Then they all agreed that peculiar was perfect.

And everyone was glad there was a different sort of piglet in the family.